THE SILVER BAYONET

CANADA

ASH BARKER

OXFORD

Published by Osprey

2023

OSPREY GAMES

OSPREY GAMES

Bloomsbury Publishing Plc

Kemp House, Chawley Park, Cumnor, Oxford, OX2 9PY, UK

29 Earlsfort Terrace, Dublin 2, Ireland

1385 Broadway, 5th Floor, New York, NY 10018, USA

E-mail: info@ospreygames.co.uk

www.ospreygames.co.uk

OSPREY GAMES is a trademark of Osprey Publishing Ltd

First published in Great Britain in 2023

A catalogue record for this book is available from the British Library.

ISBN: PB 9781472858870; eBook 9781472858900; ePDF 9781472858894; XML 9781472858887

23 24 25 26 27 10 9 8 7 6 5 4 3 2 1

Originated by PDQ Digital Media Solutions, Bungay, UK

Printed and bound in India by Replika Press Private Ltd

Osprey Games supports the Woodland Trust, the UK's leading woodland conservation charity. Between 2014 and 2018 our donations are being spent on their Centenary Woods project in the UK.

To find out more about our authors and books visit www.ospreypublishing.com. Here you will find extracts, author interviews, details of forthcoming events and the option to sign up for our newsletter.

LAND
ACKNOWLEDGEMENT

The Author acknowledges the Upper Canadian land on which this book was written is the traditional territory of the Anishinaabe and Haudenosaunee peoples, many of whom continue to live and work here today. This territory is covered by the Upper Canada Treaties and is within the land protected by the Dish With One Spoon Wampum agreement. Today, this gathering place is home to many First Nations, Métis, and Inuit peoples and acknowledging this reminds us that our great standard of living is directly related to the resources and friendship of indigenous peoples. The author is grateful for the experiences and enrichment he has benefited from throughout his personal journey with those members of the First Nations, Métis, and Inuit peoples across North America and how it has shaped his life.

To learn more:

MISSISSAUGAS OF THE CREDIT FIRST NATIONS
https://mncfn.ca/

THE ANISHINAABE
www.anishinabek.ca/education-resources/gdoo-sastamoo-kii-mi/who-are-the-anishinaabeg/

THE HAUDENOSAUNEE CONFEDERACY
www.haudenosauneeconfederacy.com/

A DISH WITH ONE SPOON
www.thecanadianencyclopedia.ca/en/article/a-dish-with-one-spoon

MAP OF ONTARIO TREATIES
www.ontario.ca/page/map-ontario-treaties-and-reserves

CONTENTS

CHAPTER ONE

INTRODUCTION

I was born in Toronto, a city built upon the banks of one of Canada's Great Lakes. These massive fresh bodies of water are almost large enough to be considered inland seas. For thousands of years, they fed the early humans and wildlife that made their home here. While early humanoid life was spreading from Africa across the world, shaping the lands of Europe and Asia, the vast expanses of North America lay mostly empty and wild.

The early pioneers of humanity that crossed over from Asia during the Ice Age found an incomprehensibly vast expanse of wilderness. For tens of thousands of years, they built lives and communities within these lands until European explorers arrived here only a few short centuries ago. They too were humbled by its enormity and utterly unprepared for the scope and power of the place. Different from those first peoples, European colonists brought with them some things that this land, in turn, was unprepared for. Industry, along with disease and politics, had grown to be powerful forces in Europe and, by the time of our story, were its primary exports.

This book is quite personal to me. My formative experiences growing up as a Canadian descendant of British, Irish, and French colonists have been in the aftermath of that tectonic cultural and environmental collision. Modern North America is a product of an enormous portion of largely untouched planet Earth, inhabited by humans mostly in harmony with it, crashed into by a different branch of humankind absolutely convinced of its manifest destiny to master every inch of creation.

The Silver Bayonet is set in the period where that conflict is raging. The Harvestmen and their desire to stoke war and strife by which to siphon negative energy further draws humanity into disagreement with the supernatural and mythological. This period of disagreement with both natural and unnatural forces is a prime setting to explore these stories.

A great many of the creatures encountered in this book come from the traditions and mythologies of First Nation Peoples from across North America and I have done my best to depict these as accurately and respectfully as possible while writing a fiction based in this period.

The lesson of the Harvestmen is that, no matter where we go, we bring our evils with us and, in our ignorance, come into conflict with things we do not understand.

THE NORTH AND THE PASSAGE

At the end of the American Revolutionary War, the North American continent was settling into a new set of borders and governments amidst a backdrop of westward expansion. For the European colonists, the continental landmass of North America was still largely unexplored and uncharted to the north and west.

The sudden revolutionary formation of the United States had also precipitated the creation of two distinct British Provinces above it, those being Upper and Lower Canada. These two regions were unique from one another both politically and socially, as they incorporated people of a variety of European heritages and indigenous nations. At the same time, the vast fortunes and influence of the various trading companies were shaping the landscape and forging semi-permanent and permanently settled communities where none might have previously existed.

These powerful trading companies have been extracting the wealth of the North since their inception. As the Napoleonic Wars continue to rage, they now also keep hard-bitten, and often strange, ex-soldiers and specialists in their employ. The trading companies own specialist units that have taken many names during the race for the Northwest Passage, but their goals have always the same; keep the river of profits flowing back eastward to line their ledgers. After all, they were the ones whose money, ships, and avarice to harvest the riches of these lands had fueled the expansion across the Atlantic for the past centuries.

The newly created Canadian provinces found themselves full of imported superstitions, faiths, cultural biases, and the scars of the American Revolutionary War. Veterans of that conflict and those of the hidden war with the Harvestmen, as well as other supernatural forces, have spread across the New World. Disbanded specialist units have found employment both with colonial militaries.

When playing a *Silver Bayonet* campaign set in Canada during this period, you can freely create a specialist unit from the main rulebook. These French Revolutionary and Napoleonic War veterans may have simply stayed together in colonial employ or are working in the interests of a Trading Company. They may even have been seconded to the British Crown or United States forces during the war, or be employed by their governments for their own ends.

You may also create new units using one of the four nations (one of which is not actually a nation, but would have had equivalent power and influence at the time) provided here. These nations are: The United States, Upper Canada, Lower Canada, and the Trading Companies.

UPPER AND LOWER CANADA

In 1791, after the American Revolutionary War had created the United States and ended British rule in the former Thirteen Colonies, the British Canadian colonies were divided into two distinct regions due to the influx of new people from the south. These 'United Empire Loyalists' desired a system of governance more in line with British Rule and settled in the Upper Canada region, which comprised most of modern Southern Ontario, extending up to the regions of Georgian Bay and Lake Superior.

Lower Canada comprised what is now the southern portion of Quebec, as well as Labrador and Newfoundland. The residents there continued to use the old French systems of governance and the majority of the population located there still natively spoke French as a first language alongside following those colonial customs.

Because the colonies differed so much in governance and culture, they can be selected as individual Nations for the purposes of a *Silver Bayonet* campaign. Both territories had imported their own superstitions and supernatural baggage to the New World from Europe, and both realised that, as the flames of war engulfed the world, some supernatural sights were set on them, the same monsters and myths that had been battled in Europe were emerging here as well.

THE UNITED STATES

Newly minted in the American Revolutionary War, the United States borders the southern edges of both Upper and Lower Canada. Tensions between the two British territories and this newly independent nation would reach a peak during the War of 1812. The various and ongoing conflicts have solidified the Harvestmen's supernatural presence, in part due to their ability to feed on the pain and suffering caused. With a firm foothold in the New World, they seek to raise tensions and rekindle war in North America to bring forth their powers in this new land.

With the British already fully aware, the War of 1812 now came with its own spectral repercussions. The American military absorbed those specialist units already loyal to their new union and put them to work as they set their eyes on the Canadian colonies for the sake of their new nation.

THE TRADING COMPANIES

While the nations of Europe and the newly formed United States played out their political dramas in North America, the hand of industry had been quietly (or not so quietly in some cases) paving the roads, building and expanding forts and waterways, and generally doing all the heavy lifting of exploring and expanding what would eventually be the vast geographic nation of Canada.

The Hudson Bay Company was originally founded by two French fur traders, but was backed by the English, and eventually British, governments and given their charter in the 17th century. This company was to eventually absorb all its rivals and dominate trade and exploration in northern North America for close to three hundred years. However, during the Napoleonic Wars, the War of 1812, and the conflict with the Harvestmen, there were numerous powerful and dynamic trading companies at war with them. With their own private military forces and assets, companies like the Northwest Trading Company or the XY Trading Company would employ their own specialist units as new battles began to rage.

CHAPTER TWO

NEW RECRUITMENT LISTS AND SOLDIERS

NEW RECRUITMENT LISTS

UPPER CANADA

Artillerist, Doctor, Discovery Serviceman, Guard, Grenadier, Highlander, Infantryman, Junior Officer, Light Cavalryman, Marine, Native Scout, Occultist, Sapper, Supernatural Investigator, Tactician, Veteran Hunter, Woodsman

LOWER CANADA

Artillerist, Champion of the Faith, Doctor, Guard, Infantryman, Junior Officer, Light Cavalryman, Loup Garou, Sailor, Native Scout, Occultist, Sailor, Supernatural Investigator, Veteran Hunter, Voyageur, Vivandiere, Woodsman

THE UNITED STATES

Artillerist, Champion of the Faith, Doctor, Grenadier, Heavy Cavalryman, Infantryman, Junior Officer, Light Cavalryman, Marine, Native Scout, Occultist, Rifleman, Sailor, Sapper, Supernatural Investigator, Veteran Hunter, Woodsman

TRADING COMPANIES

Trading Companies are unique in that they may select soldiers from the following list, but players may also decide at the creation of their Unit to add up to four additional soldier types (shown in a second list and marked with an *) in the employment of their Company. Doctor,

Grenadier, Infantryman, Junior Officer, Light Cavalryman, Native Scout, Sailor, Sapper, Supernatural Investigator, Tactician, Voyageur, Woodsman

The following soldiers are mutually exclusive, meaning that if one type is selected for your Trading Company then you cannot select either of the other two; the types are: Damphyr, Loup Garou, and Werebear.

Once you've selected these additional four soldier types they are the unique make-up of your particular Trading Company and may not be changed.

ADDITIONAL UNITS

Damphyr*, Champion of the Faith*, Discovery Serviceman*, Highlander*, Loup Garou*, Marine*, Occultist*, Veteran Hunter*, Werebear*

NEW SOLDIERS

DISCOVERY SERVICEMAN

Nationalities: Upper Canada, Trading Companies

While technically an arm of the British Navy, the explorers of the Discovery Service were often funded by the trading companies. This was in a desperate effort to chart a passage through the Arctic to secure a vital trade route to Asia. The advantages this had was that it would be shorter than the traditional routes being used at the time. This obsession would lead to hundreds of deaths, lost ships, and madness as these expeditions battled both the natural and supernatural elements of the North to chase this elusive dream. Veterans of these expeditions are both reliable and steady-minded, and in high demand for specialist units.

DISCOVERY SERVICEMAN						
Speed	Melee	Accuracy	Defence	Courage	Health	Recruitment
6	+1	+1	13	+1	12	18
Attributes: Expert Climber, Steady Legs						
Equipment: Hand Weapon, Blunderbuss, Pistol, Shotbag						

LOUP GAROU

Nationalities: Lower Canada, Trading Companies

Those men cursed with lycanthropy, or 'mad wolves' as the French would call them, would often have a hard time finding employment when their condition became known. It makes sense that a great many would journey to the New World, taking this affliction with them. Those with their affliction under control could often find a place in a specialist unit, where their powerful wolf-forms could do battle with the supernatural entities at large in the New World.

When in Wolf form, the Loup Garou gains +1 Melee, +2 Courage, Strong, Damage Reduction (5), Nimble, Quick, and Master of Cover, but can no longer use a firearm or investigate clue markers.

LOUP GAROU						
Speed	Melee	Accuracy	Defence	Courage	Health	Recruitment
6	+2	+0	14	+1	14	30
Attributes: Skinshift (Wolf), Allergy (Silver and Fire), Quick Heal,						
Equipment: Hand Weapon, Pistol						

VOYAGEUR

Nationalities: Lower Canada, Trading Companies

Attracted by the promises of adventure and held in massively high regard in local folklore, the majority of voyageurs were employed as guides and laborers in the fur-trade boom of the seventeenth and eighteenth century. To be a voyageur you had to be capable of carrying two 90lb (41kg) bundles of furs on a five mile portage, at a minimum. These intimidating frontiersmen were both tremendously strong and massively in demand for their skill and ability.

VOYAGEUR						
Speed	Melee	Accuracy	Defence	Courage	Health	Recruitment
6	+1	+1	14	+1	10	20
Attributes: Steady Legs, Strong						
Equipment: Hand Weapon, Rifle, Cartridge Box						

WOODSMAN

Nationalities: Upper Canada, Lower Canada, United States, Trading Companies

Great forests cover vast areas of North America. The men who inhabit these forests are tough survivalists. While they often lack any formal military training, their skills at hunting, foraging, forest-craft, and orienteering can often prove useful in specialist units. Above anything else, woodsmen know about fire and can quickly start fires when they are needed.

WOODSMAN						
Speed	Melee	Accuracy	Defence	Courage	Health	Recruitment
6	+1	+1	13	+0	10	15
Attributes: Nimble, Fire-Starter						
Equipment: Rifle, Cartridge Box						

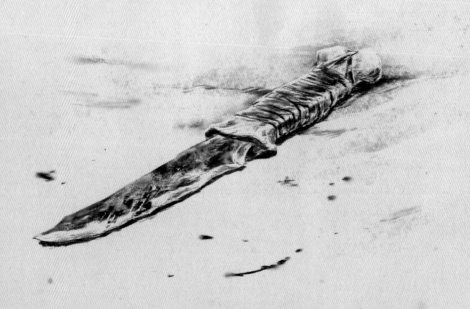

CHAPTER THREE

ADVENTURES IN THE NORTH

The following five scenarios represent common clashes between specialist units in Upper and Lower Canada during the Napoleonic Wars and the War of 1812. Whether in royal or government employ, or at the behest of one of the trading companies whose agendas dominated most power struggles in the region, they can be played out in order or at random by rolling on the Canada Scenario Table.

CANADA SCENARIO TABLE	
D10	Scenario
1–2	Trade Routes
3–4	The Outpost
5–6	Wings of Sleep
7–8	The Serpent's Curse
9–10	1812 Overture

When playing any scenario (including the solo campaign presented later) in the Canadian colonies, you may use the Unexpected Events table in the main rulebook as normal, with one exception. Unless playing the Scenario 5: 1812 Overture, re-roll any results of Artillery Strike.

Alternatively, you may use the Unexpected Encounters rules as normal, but roll on the Canadian Colonies Unexpected Encounters table presented here instead of the one in *The Silver Bayonet* main rulebook.

CANADIAN COLONIES UNEXPECTED ENCOUNTERS	
Die Roll	Encounter
1	Demon (*The Silver Bayonet*, page 140)
2	Grizzly Bear (see page 53)
3	'Timber Wolf' aka Dark Wolf (*The Silver Bayonet*, page 139)
4	'Loup Garou' aka Werewolf (*The Silver Bayonet*, page 146)
5	Bandit (*The Silver Bayonet*, page 137)
6	'Cannibal' aka Ghoul (*The Silver Bayonet*, page 141)
7	Revenant (*The Silver Bayonet*, page 145)
8	Moose (see page 56)
9	Harvestman Agent (see page 55)
10	'Spirit' aka Ghost (*The Silver Bayonet*, page 140)

In order to not spoil the details of the scenarios for those that wish to play them in order, and particularly for the solo campaign, here is a list of models that will be featured throughout the missions in this supplement. It also includes all the models in the Canadian Colonies Encounter Table should you wish to use it.

- 1 Bandit: possibly a deserter or lone hunter or trapper.
- 1 Baxbaxwalanuskiwe: an ogre sized monster, completely covered in snapping mouths.
- 1 Demon: any angry supernatural agent would work well for this.
- 4–6 Ghouls: colonists driven to cannibalism.
- 3 Ghosts
- 1 Grizzly Bear
- 1 Harvestman Agent: A sorcerous agent of the Harvestmen.
- 1 Harvestman Assassin: A face-changing agent of the Harvestmen.
- 1 Moose
- 2 Polar Bears
- 1 Revenant
- 1 Timber Wolf
- 1 Tsemaus: a river and lake monster that disguises itself as floating logs and trees.
- 1 Wendigo: a massive, emaciated supernatural horror driven by an endless hunger.
- 1 Werewolf

SCENARIO 1:
TRADE ROUTES

Unlike Europe, Canada has yet to be crisscrossed by thousands of years of roadbuilding. Because of that, the waterways that naturally flow back out to the sea, and therefore Europe, are vital highways for moving goods overland to port and market.

Your unit has been making their way west as instructed when you come upon the wreckage of canoes, pelts, and clothing floating down-river towards you. While misadventure is common this far from settled territory, it isn't until what looks like bobbing limbs begin to appear amongst the wreckage that something seems to be afoot. Other travelers can be seen ahead on the shoreline, but how could they have produced such carnage so suddenly? Pulling your boats to the opposite side of the shore, you shout across a warning as you look to investigate. Clearly, something strange is happening. Perhaps the land itself is angered at the men littering its arteries with their petty wars and has sent one of its agents in response?

SET-UP

This scenario should be played on a 2.5' x 2.5' table. A river runs through the middle 18" of the table, running top to bottom. Place four large logjams at four equal points on the river, starting from near the top edge of the table and ending near the bottom. Each logjam should be roughly 3" in radius. In the centre of each, place a clue marker.

The left and right sides of the table should be thickly wooded with occasional rocks. Boats can be pulled ashore within a 6" of the top left and bottom right corners of the table.

A number of pieces of floating wreckage may also be placed in the river, which provide cover to any models in the water.

Both players should roll a die. The player who rolls the highest should deploy their unit wholly within 10" of either the top left or bottom right corner. The other player then deploys their entire force wholly within 10" of the other specified corner.

SPECIAL RULES

The entire river counts as difficult ground apart from the logjams. Models can walk on the logjams normally provided the soldier first passes a TN10 Movement test. If this test is failed, the logjam still counts as difficult terrain and is an unsteady platform for firing rifles. Models with Steady Legs do not need to take this test.

In addition, if any model dives for cover while within the river, roll a die. On a result of a 1 or 2, their powder is soaked for the duration of the game and they may no longer fire their ranged weapons. Any model attempting to reload a firearm in the river must also roll a die. On a 1 or 2, the action fails as their weapon fouls, but it may be attempted again during a following turn.

Once the Tsemaus (page 57) has revealed itself, remove it from the river at the end of each turn. During the following turn, at the start of the Monster Phase, place it 5" away from a random model still in the river that has any received any wounds. If no wounded models are

in the river, place it next to a random, unwounded model instead. If no models are in the river, it will not surface.

The game ends when one unit has no soldiers remaining or has entirely fled the table.

TRADE ROUTES CLUE MARKER TABLE	
Card	Clue
Ace of Spades	Tsemaus: Place a Tsemaus (page 57) at the edge of the logjam, as close as possible to the investigating figure. It will attack this figure during the Monster Phase using the Lunge ability regardless of range.
King of Spades	Savaged Corpse: Monstrous jaws have torn a man to pieces and parts of the body are trapped by the movement of the water against the flotsam. This figure must make a Terror Check (-1). Gain 1 Fate Die.
Queen of Spades	Storm Lantern: A lit storm lantern on a pole still sticks up from the churning river. The model now carrying it may make a single shooting attack at a range of 6" with a +2 modifier to hit causing Fire damage, then the Storm Lantern is lost.
Jack of Spades	Trade Map: A map annotated with notes on the reported issues that may be encountered when navigating the river. Also has various scribblings and stories about a great beast that disguises itself amongst the debris and wreckage of failed expeditions. Gain 1 Skill Die.

REWARDS

Units receive the following bonus experience points for this scenario:

- +1 experience point if the unit investigates two or more clue markers.
- +1 experience point if the unit has figures still on the table when the game ends.
- +1 experience point if a unit ends the game in possession of the Trade Map.
- +2 experience points if the unit kills the Tsemaus.

SCENARIO 2:
THE OUTPOST

Company forts have long been used as stepping stonest o keep the trade routes running from the deep wilderness back to civilization. These waystations can range from tiny outposts ringed in rough-cut log walls to sprawling installations where hundreds of people toil away as grist to the machine of industry. Hundreds of miles can separate these communities and they are frequently on their own for months at a time. Reports of their doings are diligently fed back through the company networks. However, when one goes quiet for too long, a unit is usually sent out to investigate. If that unit doesn't return, a more specialized team is then tasked with discovering what has happened, lest the company's stocks be looted or its competitors gain some foothold in the area.

Yours is one such unit, tasked with discovering the fate of a place north of the Great Lakes with the ironic and unfitting name of Providence. The previous autumn, the company custodians there were last reported to be low on grain, tobacco, and medicine, with the rocky landscape of the area unsuitable for growing their own food. A harsh winter left them without any new provisions and no word has come from them since.

As your unit, along with others, heads north to check on these communities, you hear dark rumors at other outposts that something terrible has happened there and that local trappers now refuse to trade with them. There are also stories of other company men being mustered to deal with the problem. Your superiors will want to know the reason for this, so you set off to investigate.

As you arrive in the clearing, the sun begins to set. You see figures moving inside the now decrepit looking fort, one of whom seems to be in the midst of processing game. You appear not to be the first to arrive, however, and a warning rings out across the forest's edge as you advance.

SET-UP

This scenario should be played on a 3' x 3' table. In centre of the table set up a small wilderness fort. There should be entrances at the top and bottom, and small outbuildings within the walls. A central building no bigger than 6" across should be placed in the middle of the table. The entire fort should fill an area roughly 16" in diameter. Place two clue markers inside the fort along the centerline of the table, each roughly 5" in from the left and right edges of the fort.

The area 6" around the fort is clear-cut but can be strewn with the discarded junk, piled logs or hung furs that support the encampment, providing cover. Place a clue marker outside the north and south entrances to the fort, 4" outside.

The edges of the table should be wooded with low-lying cover interspersed.

Inside the fort, place four ghouls (*The Silver Bayonet*, page 141) in contact with the four corners of the central structure.

Both players should roll a die. The player who rolls the highest should deploy their unit wholly within 3" of either the top or bottom table edge. The other player then deploys their entire force wholly within 3" of the other edge.

SPECIAL RULES

The Ghouls will not exit the perimeter of the fort, instead attempting to move out of line of sight of all soldiers until a soldier enters the walls. They will then operate as normal monsters.

At the beginning of the second turn, start marking a Hunger score. Each time a Ghoul or soldier is killed, add 1 to the Hunger score. When the Hunger score reaches 12 or more, the Baxbaxwalanuksiwe (see page 46) immediately explodes from a random side of the central building and then behaves as normal monster for the rest of the game.

The game ends when one unit has no soldiers remaining or has entirely fled the table.

THE OUTPOST CLUE MARKER TABLE	
Card	Clue
Ace of Spades	Human Remains: What has been done to the body of this man is unspeakable. This figure must make a Terror Check (-1). Add 1 Fate Die to your pool.
King of Spades	An Open Fire with Cookpot: After a long week of traveling the meal looks almost appetising, until you spot the finger in the pot. Add 1 Fate Die to your pool.
Queen of Spades	A Journal of Insane Ramblings: The fate of the men seems to have come to them in the dead of winter as they were starving. A cursory look at the book indicates they have made a pact with some spirit in the woods that promised them survival at a terrible cost. Add 1 Power Die to your pool. If the investigating figure moves off the table, the Journal has been secured. The figure may drop the journal during its activation without spending an action, and automatically drops it if reduced to 0 Health. In this case, mark the Journal's location on the table. Any figure adjacent to the Journal may pick it up by spending an action, so long as no enemy figures are within 1" of it.
Jack of Spades	A Burn Pit: The clothing and belongings of dozens of other travellers appears to have been disposed of here. These unlucky few were unaware of the change in the fort. This need for caution gives you some insight into the weaknesses of the creatures here and their dislike of being exposed. Add 1 Skill Die to your pool.

REWARDS

Units receive the following bonus experience points for this scenario:

- +1 experience points if you investigate two or more clue markers.
- +1 experience point if your unit destroys two or more Ghouls.
- +1 experience point if you end the game with a model in possession of the Journal.
- +3 experience points if you end the game having destroyed the manifestation of Baxbaxwalanuksiwe.

SCENARIO 3:
WINGS OF SLEEP

Your unit has received reports from travellers that the region you are about to enter is possibly haunted. Strange, vivid dreams and flitting shadows seem to stalk the unwary and stories even tell of folk finding themselves asleep on the trail, waking mid-day or later, and even being found by others half-devoured while still in their blankets. This route has been deemed of the utmost importance to the company and ordered secured at all costs by your superiors, so, as the leaves begin to turn, you set off west to chase down whether the rumours are idle gossip or if something more sinister that haunts these woods.

Not a week from your current outpost, you find signs of a clearing that appears to be often used as a place for rest by travellers. There are the remains of a destroyed cook fire, ashes scattered, and what appear to be bones are strewn everywhere. You hear a shout from ahead as another group approaches with anger in their voices, clearly of the mind that your unit must be involved in some way.

SET-UP

This scenario should be played on a 2.5' x 2.5' table. A trail should wind from top to bottom through the middle of the table. On the left side, an encampment with a cook-fire, supplies, and scattered belongings should take up a roughly 10" diameter circle set on the horizontal midline. To the right side, a cave entrance should be set on that same line, 8" from the pathway.

The rest of the table should be wooded, with rocky outcroppings and scrub.

Place two clue markers on the top and bottom edges of the encampment and one next to the destroyed cook fire. Then place one in the centre of the table on the path and one at the mouth of the cave.

Both players should roll a die. The player who rolls the highest should deploy their unit wholly within 3" of either the top or bottom table edge. The other player then deploys their entire force wholly within 3" of the other edge.

SPECIAL RULES

Unknown to the units, the area has become infested with the spirits of Wingoc. These are huge supernatural moths that force sentient beings to sleep and then feed on their dreams.

This has become particularly problematic for the sleepers, as a huge grizzly bear has now decided to make its den nearby this seemingly limitless supply of food as it puts on fat for the winter.

Beginning with the start of the Monster Phase on Turn 2, the model furthest from another soldier (either friendly or enemy) for each player must take a TN10 Courage test as the Wingocs are roused to their presence and swarm them with their soporific magic. If they fail, they will fall into a deep and supernatural sleep. Place a die next to every sleeping model at the beginning of each subsequent Monster Phase, marked with a 1. This is the penalty to the Courage of that figure for the remainder of the game as their dreams are fed upon. Should the Courage of a figure ever drop to a negative number because of this, they are taken out of action but do not suffer an injury roll after the game.

Any friendly figure in contact with a sleeping model may attempt to rouse them by spending an action and succeeding at a TN7 Courage Test. They immediately wake but only have a single action to activate with later in that turn. Any penalty to their Courage remains until the end of the game.

The game ends when one unit has no awake soldiers remaining or has entirely fled the table.

WINGS OF SLEEP CLUE MARKER TABLE	
Card	Clue
Ace of Spades	Grizzly Bear: The noise and confusion has roused the bear from its den. Place the Bear (see 53) at the mouth of the cave and add 1 Fate Die to your pool.
King of Spades	Wingoc Nest: This figure must immediately test to resist falling asleep as per the Special Rules above.
Queen of Spades	Dreamcatcher: This talisman seems to offer some protection from the spirits here. Roll three dice and select the highest two results when resisting the Wingoc.
Jack of Spades	Wingoc Nest: This figure must immediately test to resist falling asleep as per the Special Rules above.
10 of Spades	Huge Tracks: Clearly, a bear has been feeding in this area, its tracks are all through the path and clearing. You feel better equipped now that you know the physical threat. Add 1 Skill Die to your pool.

REWARDS

Units receive the following bonus experience points for this scenario:

- +1 experience points if your unit investigates three or more clue markers.
- +1 experience if two or more members of a unit successfully resist a Wingoc swarm.
- +1 experience if your unit kills three or more enemy figures..
- +1 experience if your unit successfully wakes a friendly figure.
- +2 experience if your unit kills the Grizzly Bear.

SCENARIO 4:
THE SERPENT'S CURSE

Harvestmen agents are just as much a threat to both federal and company interests and their use of dark magics to subvert or incite conflict amongst the major players in the region is something special units constantly have to contend with.

A courier has sent word to your superiors that rival forces have somehow caused an outbreak of disease in an outpost your unit is visiting, and the higher-ups have marched forces into the wilderness to investigate the truth of that claim. Upon arrival they discover the "enemy" already in the outpost, seemingly looting the place for all it is worth.

The reality is that your unit was simply attempting to trade and resupply at the waystation, but found some calamity of unnatural wasting has befallen the place, the victims seemingly aging hundreds of years overnight. The agent that caused this must still be here somewhere, and you now have the unenviable task of both defending yourselves from the investigating forces and hunting down the culprit! The pale and drawn faces of survivors can be seen looking furtively through the windows, but you have no idea who the perpetrator could be.

SET-UP

This scenario should be played on a 2.5' x 2.5' table. The majority of the table should be set up with appropriate buildings (at least three) and scattered small terrain to represent an early 19th century outpost. The outskirts should be forested with light scattering of rough terrain, representing the nearby wilderness. No buildings should be placed within 4" of the centre of the table, but some small light obstacles may be there to provide cover.

Place five clue markers in an evenly distributed circle, 10" from the centre of the table, ideally with each in contact with a piece of terrain.

Both players should roll a die. The player that rolls the lowest deploys their entire unit within 4" of the centre of the table.

The player that rolls higher divides their unit into two groups as evenly as possible. One group deploys within 3" of the top table edge, while the other deploys within 3" of the bottom table edge.

SPECIAL RULES

The Harvestman Agent that infiltrated the outpost is still hiding in the vicinity and must be caught. This is in order to prove that your force was not responsible for the deaths of the outpost inhabitants.

The various clue markers on the table tell the sorry tale of what befell the inhabitants here and must be collected to prove which of the survivors huddling inside the buildings is the Harvestman Agent.

When a player's Investigation score reaches six, or the final clue marker is revealed, the Harvestman Agent (page 55) is placed in base contact with a building closest to the clue marker that triggered their appearance, as they realise they have been found out. They will attempt to escape towards the nearest deployment edge, moving their full distance and then attempting to Curse anyone nearby. They will move off the battlefield if able, at which point they are considered to have escaped.

To cover their escape, they will spit a cowardly curse at the nearest soldier to where they appear. This is an Accuracy +3 attack, which can be reacted to as normal. It causes no damage, but that soldier takes 1 point of Damage each time they activate from now on as the curse draws out their life. If the Agent is not slain, then the soldier must make an injury roll at the conclusion of the scenario.

The game ends when one unit has no soldiers remaining or has entirely fled the table.

THE SERPENT'S CURSE CLUE MARKER TABLE	
Card	Clue
Ace of Spades	Camp Manager's Journal: The stories of arrivals and departures give you a number of names. Earn D3 Investigation Points.
King of Spades	Quartermaster's Inventory: The ledger of checked out goods reveals some odd requests over the past weeks. Earn D3 Investigation Points.
Queen of Spades	Strange Fish: A traveller's trunk seems to have the remains of a strange fish encased in a lead-sleeved box. It has an identification plate screwed to it. Earn D3 Investigation Points.
Jack of Spades	Odd Stew: While the camp is quite distant from any major source of fish, what appears to be a small amount of fish stew has been prepared, but only served at one of the meals recently. Earn D5 Investigation Points.
King of Spades	Strange Book: A tome chronicling the early travels of a Jesuit missionary that tells of strange tales about the local wildlife. Earn D5 Investigation Points.

REWARDS

Units receive the following bonus experience points for this scenario:

- +2 experience points if your unit earns five or more Investigation Points over the course of the Scenario.
- +1 experience point if your unit reveals the clue marker that identifies the Harvestman Agent.
- +1 experience point if your unit kills the Harvestman Agent.
- +1 experience if your unit kills three or more enemy figures.

SCENARIO 5:
1812 OVERTURE

Another war between the British colonies to the north and the newly formed United States to the south was inevitable given the outcome of the American Revolutionary War. The Harvestmen's emergence in the New World was precipitated by this violence, and their agents did much to propagate aggression between nations to further expand their growing power.

With raids across the borders and the silencing of watch-forts, patrols prepare for covert actions to catch messengers and bedevilled specialist units in the New World whose employers often find themselves unwittingly doing the bidding of those malevolent forces trying to spark a full-scale war.

Two specialist units have found themselves at odds but neither suspect that the other has actually been infiltrated by an agent of the Harvestmen. Their goal is to slay the Officer leading the other force.

SET-UP

Set up the battlefield to represent a well-travelled road running top to bottom through the centre, with undeveloped woodlands or pasture to either side and scattered trees and rocks. Place a clue marker in the centre of the battlefield.

Both players should roll a die. The player who rolls the highest should deploy their unit wholly within 3" of either the top or bottom table edge. The other player then deploys their entire force wholly within 3" of the other edge.

Each player should then take it in turns to place two more clue markers each (for a total of five), next to an opposing (non-Officer) soldier.

SPECIAL RULES

One of the soldiers marked with a clue marker is, in fact, a Harvestman Assassin (page 55), sent to kill the opposing Officer. Whenever a soldier with a clue marker is hit by a ranged or melee attack, reveal that Clue.

The Central clue marker may only be revealed by an Officer. If it is, one of the remaining soldiers with a clue marker is randomly selected to be the Harvestman Assassin. The Assassin will target the Officer leading the opposing unit. They will now attack as a monster, always moving towards their target if possible.

If that Officer is already slain, the Harvestman Assassin immediately retreats to the nearest top or bottom table edge, moving and throwing Curses, as well as fighting in Melee if necessary.

The soldier replaced by the Assassin is found later, bound and gagged but otherwise none the worse for wear.

The game ends when one unit has no soldiers remaining or has entirely fled the table.

1812 OVERTURE CLUE MARKER TABLE	
Card	Clue
Ace of Spades	Nothing Suspicious: This soldier is not the Assassin.
King of Spades	Reacts Normally: This soldier is not the Assassin.
Queen of Spades	Leaps into the Fght: This soldier is not the Assassin.
Jack of Spades	The Air Shimmers as if a Cloud Has Passed in Front of the Sun: The Harvestman Assassin is revealed and leaps forward towards its prey, spitting curses in a language older than man's arrival in the New World. Once this clue marker has been revealed, all unrevealed clue markers should be removed from the table.

REWARDS

Units receive the following bonus experience points for this scenario:

- +1 experience points if your Officer was the Harvestman Assassin's target and survives the scenario.
- +1 experience point if your unit reveals the clue that identifies the Harvestman Assassin.
- +1 experience point if your unit kills the Harvestman Assassin.
- +1 experience point if your unit had the soldier impersonated by the Harvestman Assassin.
- +1 experience point if your unit kills three or more enemy figures.

CHAPTER FOUR

THE LONG NIGHT: A SOLO CAMPAIGN

Various expeditions have attempted to navigate the endless ice flows, rocky shores, and long nights of the Arctic Circle. Those still there when winter finally locks the waters in their icy grip are forced to endure a terrifying endless night. The ice slowly shifts around their ships, grinding the hull like a huge vice with its constant movement. As the ice forms beneath the hull, ships can start to list and many were eventually broken as their starving and terrified crew sheltered helplessly within.

Your unit was seconded to one such ship in the employ of the Discovery Service. In the brass message capsules of the previous expedition, sights were reported of strange lights prior to the crew's disappearance. Your unit was tasked with rescue, if possible, but it is now deep into the winter and your own ship has become locked in the ice flows south of King William Island.

As you were equipped for rescue and not to winter over on the ice, food has become scarce and the crew fractious and unruly. The captain has tasked your unit with scouting a route overland to the south, to escape the howling winds and reach the relative safety of a location where cabins can be built and food hunted. Having found a route off the ice, your unit returns in the midst a growing storm to find a massacre aboard your ice-locked vessel. The remaining food has been stolen, officers and crew slaughtered, and a large number of your former shipmates have struck out on their own.

Your only hope for survival now rests in tracking these mutineers down and determining what actually transpired. You've little hope of building a camp to survive the remainder of winter without the remaining foodstuffs they have stolen.

> This solo campaign is designed to be challenging and is best played through by an experienced Silver Bayonet unit. It is intended to be attempted by veterans of the supernatural Napoleonic Wars who have come into the employ of the Discovery Service due to their expertise.

CAMPAIGN SPECIAL RULES

This campaign uses all the solo play rules from *The Silver Bayonet* main rulebook, with the following additions:

HUNGER

At the beginning of the campaign, your unit has been marching across the ice on a reconnaissance mission for the ship's captain. Supplies are already low and one of your party is complaining about their empty belly as you come within sight of the ship. Randomly select a unit member to gain the Hunger condition. Hungry models may not sprint and become distracted and weak-handed. Every time they take the Reload action, roll a D10. On the roll of a 1, they drop their powder or otherwise spoil the load – the action is lost and the weapon remains unloaded.

After each scenario of the campaign, you may scavenge for game and then must feed your unit. The unit begins with 5 Provisions. As long as at least one soldier survived the encounter, you may scavenge the battlefield and the surrounding area to add an additional 1D10 Provisions to your stockpile. Every soldier you do not feed a Provision to at the end of the scenario will be marked as Hungry. As the campaign takes place over only a few days, there are no additional effects for missing more than a single meal in a row.

You may find additional Provisions throughout the scenarios. If you do so, mark them on your Unit Roster. They are carried collectively by the group so it is not required for them to be given to any particular soldier.

CASUALTIES

In the vast void of the Canadian Arctic, you will have no opportunity to recruit new soldiers to your cause until you escape back to more populated lands. Any soldier killed in action may not be replaced until the end of the Campaign.

SCENARIO 1:
ESCAPE FROM THE ICE

The trail is quickly being obscured by the storm blowing across the ice from the northwest. As you make your way after the mutineers, you realise that there are shapes moving out amongst the jagged ice floes.

You must race to follow them and secure the remaining supplies if you are to survive a journey off the ice and downriver to the mainland. If you cannot catch up to them in time, you will most likely starve before you can reach somewhere with enough wildlife to sustain your unit.

SET-UP

The table should be set up with jagged rocks and icy crags dotting the table. This should make the path to the opposite edge fairly difficult to navigate in a straight line. Set up a single clue marker in the centre of the table. Set up four additional clue markers within 6" of the centreline of the table and at least 6" from any other clue markers.

Your unit should deploy within 3" of the bottom of the bottom edge, heading towards the top.

SPECIAL RULES

As blowing snow blinds the soldiers, all Shooting Attacks will be at a -2 Accuracy. This is except for Blunderbusses whose indiscriminate nature does not require such precision.

Do not remove clue markers when they have been searched in this scenario. Rather, flip them over or mark them in some way to denote that you cannot search them again.

Whenever a clue marker is searched, roll a D10. On a roll of 6 or more, one of the enraged Polar Bears emerges from the storm to attack the party. Place a Polar Bear (page 57) within 1" of a random clue marker. A maximum of two Polar Bears are revealed in this way. If two have not been revealed by the time the final clue marker is searched, they both arrive automatically. Whenever a Polar Bear is wounded, there is a chance it will retreat into the storm. Roll a D10 at the end of the Player Phase the same turn it is wounded. On a roll of 1–4 remove it from the table and heal it 1 Health as it licks its wounds. Place it next to a random clue marker at the start of the following turn's Monster Phase as it once more ambushes the unit.

The game ends when the unit has found the Strange Tracks leading south and can follow them after the mutineers. Once this clue has been discovered, the surviving unit members may exit the table by the top table edge and the scenario ends.

ESCAPE FROM THE ICE CLUE MARKER TABLE	
Card	Clue
Ace of Spades	Mutilated Corpse: The remains of one of the mutinous crew, torn apart in a grotesque fashion. Massive paw prints are everywhere at the site. This figure must make a Terror Check (-1). Gain a Monster Die.
King of Spades	Wrecked Sledge: The remains of a sledge half sunk into what appears to be the bone-scattered den of some massive animal. Did the crew thoughtlessly disturb something? There are some preserved goods still on the sledge. Gain 2 Provisions.
Queen of Spades	Dropped Rucksack: Abandoned in the snow, this was seemingly tossed aside as someone fled. Gain 1 Provision.
Jack of Spades	Slain Polar Bear Cub: It seems that the mutineers disturbed the slumber of a family of these great white bears and slew one of their young. Gain 1 Monster Die.
Ten of Spades	Strange Tracks: These do not seem like the tracks of a bear or a man. You find them next to a scene of blood and fighting, and they follow the boot prints of the crew out of the area, leading south. Gain 1 Skill Die.

REWARDS

Units receive the following bonus experience points for this scenario:

- +1 Experience points for investigating four or more clue markers.
- +2 Experience and +2 Provisions for each Polar Bear slain by your unit.
- +1 Experience for discovering both the Sledge and the Rucksack.
- +1 Experience if six or more soldiers exit the Battlefield.

SCENARIO 2: FALSE HOPE

The strange tracks lead to the shoreline. Thankful to be off the ice, and on what seems to be a large landmass, you feel hope swell as you see the outline of what looks like a roughly built cabin. As the sun sets and the storm moves off to the east, the temperatures plummet and you rush to see if your fortunes have delivered you to an unknown outpost.

The state of the cabin immediately leaves you in dismay. The door hangs loose on its hinges and there are no obvious footprintsin the freshly fallen snow apart from those of your duplicitous crewmates. It seems this shelter has been abandoned, but why did the mutineers not take advantage of a perfectly good place to wait out the storm?

Warily, you approach the structure as green lights begin to dance above you in the pitiless, starry sky.

SET-UP

The central feature of the table should be a roughly built cabin made of sappy tree poles, roughly 12" across at its widest point. Simple in design, it should contain three rooms: a main room, a storeroom, and sleeping quarters. A single open door should face the soldiers towards the bottom edge. Place this building in the centre of the table. Towards the top edge of the table, you can scatter trees as the woods encroach on the shoreline, while the bottom edge should have jagged ice flows and a rocky shoreline.

Place a red clue marker in each room of the cabin and three black clue markers 6" away from the cabin and within 3" of the centreline of the Table.

Your unit should deploy within 3" of the bottom edge of the table, along the shoreline.

SPECIAL RULES

Do not create a deck for the red clue markers. Instead, consult the appropriate room on the chart below. For the black clue markers, create a deck as normal.

Each time one of the red clue markers in the cabin is searched, a ghost (see *The Silver Bayonet*, page 140) is placed immediately at the centre of a different, random table edge. Their target point is always the nearest soldier, regardless of line of sight.

The party may exit into the forest on the top table edge once the Strange Tracks have been found and all three rooms of the cabin have been searched. The scenario is over when all surviving unit members leave the table.

FALSE HOPE RED CLUE MARKER TABLE	
Room	Clue
Main Room	Torn Journal:. The original occupants of this cabin were part of a whaling vessel's crew that became damaged and tried to winter here. Already sick from starvation, the journal describes strange visitations and dreams as the whalers began to die from lack of food. Gain 1 Skill Die.
Storeroom	Rotting Gore: As quickly as you open the door to the storeroom, you wish you had not. Human remains moulder in a corner and there are obvious signs of butchery. This figure must make a Terror Check (-1). Gain a Monster Die.
Sleeping Quarters	Ransacked Room: Obviously long abandoned, it looks as though someone has recently and hastily searched these quarters and fled. All of the bedding has been stolen or spoiled, but wedged between the wall and a shattered bunk you find a silver crucifix. All of the soldier's attacks count as Blessed for the remainder of the scenario.

FALSE HOPE BLACK CLUE MARKER TABLE	
Card	Clue
Ace of Hearts	Eerie Vision: For a moment, in the darkness you believe you can see a figure, but it disappears as you approach. A sad voice whispers in your mind that you should hurry on and that this place is cursed by what the men here did to one another. Gain a Monster Die.
King of Hearts	Strange Tracks: You discover the booted prints of the mutineers, once again fleeing south into the woods. Whatever they found here so terrified them that they ran even with the prospect of shelter. Once again, the enormous tracks seem to follow after the duplicitous crew. Gain 1 Skill Die.
Queen of Hearts	Dead Sailor: Frozen with an expression of abject terror on their face, you find one of the mutineers curled up in a terrified ball in the snow. A sack at their belt contains a few bits of unspoiled food. Gain 2 Provisions.

REWARDS

Units receive the following bonus experience points for this scenario:

- +1 experience points if five or more clue markers were investigated.

- +1 experience point for each Ghost banished and slain.

- +1 experience point if three or more soldiers exit the battlefield.

- +1 experience point if six or more soldiers exit the battlefield.

SCENARIO 3:
OPEN WATER

The mutineers' tracks lead away from the shoreline and deeper into the woodlands, climbing up the rocky escarpment that borders the sea to the north. After a cold night camped as far from the cursed cabin as you dared push, you renew your pursuit. Luckily, the dragging of the boats and sledges up the escarpment and through the frozen underbrush has left clear signs of the mutineers' passing. You and your unit are easily able to track the sailors as the wan morning sun lights the woods.

As you continue your journey, stranger and stranger scenes mark the passing of the remaining crew, including what looks like signs of fighting. Discarded clothing and bloody, crushed snow speaks of some type of violence beginning to happen within the group of traitorous men.

As you begin to hear rushing water ahead, something more ominous reaches your ears… the sounds of ripping and chewing.

You emerge into a small clearing, the boats and supplies strewn about from some terrible battle at the edge of a frozen river heading south. Hunched amongst the massacred piles of human remains is a massive horned figure, surrounded by the degenerate forms of several mutineers, all feasting on the remains of the other men.

SET-UP

Set up the table with a clearing in the centre of the table and progressively more dense woodlands to the edges. A frozen river to the upper left exits the area. The boats, currently atop the sledges, are at the river's edge and along with piles of supplies.

Place a Wendigo (see page 58). Place three Ghouls (see *The Silver Bayonet*, page 141) within 3" of it. Next, place three clue markers in a circle, each 10" from the middle of the table and roughly equally spaced

The unit deploys within 3" of the bottom table edge.

SPECIAL RULES

The Wendigo, which has been tracking the mutineers and drove them mad with hunger in the first place, has finally broken the minds of the remaining sailors. It is currently feasting upon the corpses of the other mutineers with the Ghouls that their comrades have become. Your surviving soldiers must defeat all the monsters in order to claim the boats and remaining food scattered about the clearing and begin the long march to open water along the frozen river.

OPEN WATER CLUE MARKER TABLE	
Card	Clue
Ace of Spades	Suspicious Meat: A blazing bonfire is still burning with chunks of suspicious-looking meat cooking on a spit. The soldier may grab a crude torch from the flames to be additionally equipped with a flaming hand weapon for the remainder of the scenario.
King of Spades	Medallion of Saint Christopher: It seems as though one of the less insane and more devout mutineers made a final stand here, a medallion of Saint Christopher is clutched in their fist. This soldier counts all of their attacks as Blessed for the remainder of the scenario.
Queen of Spades	Oil Cask: A small cask of oil lays here, a rag stuffed into its spigot. It could be fashioned into a crude bomb. This soldier may make a single Ranged Attack at +2 Accuracy with the Fire trait and using the Power Die for Damage.

REWARDS

Units receive the following bonus experience points for this scenario:

- +1 Experience Point for each Ghoul killed.
- +3 Experience Point for killing the Wendigo.
- +1 Experience Point if three or more soldiers survive the scenario.
- +2 Experience Points if six or more soldiers survive the scenario.

ENDING THE CAMPAIGN

After defeating the vile creature and its degenerate minions, your unit takes stock of the scene. Having inspected the remains, it all be comes clear...

It seems that at least one, possibly many, of the mutineers had come under the whispering, hungering influence of a malevolent Wendigo spirit while trapped in the ship. Having hopefully destroyed or, at the very least, banished it, your Officer and soldiers gather up the remaining food supplies, the sledges, and the small boats and begin the pull southwards towards running rivers and the possibility of an outpost to wait out the remaining winter, or, at the very least, game to sustain your group.

Thankful for having escaped the ice and the strange things abroad there, you brace yourselves for another long, cold march as the strange green lights once again begin to laughingly dance in the darkening sky.

CHAPTER FIVE

BESTIARY
NEW MONSTERS

BAXBAXWALANUKSIWE

This spirit has many names, ranging from "Cannibal-at-the-North-End-of-the-world' to 'He-who-first-ate-Man-at-the-Mouth-of-the-River". His massive, eyeless form is bearlike but without fur and entirely covered in snapping jaws that chant "BAK! BAK! BAK!" ("Eat! Eat! Eat!"). Much like hunger itself, he will always return to tempt living souls who are without food, but can be banished for a time.

BAXBAXWALANUKSIWE						
Speed	Melee	Accuracy	Defence	Courage	Health	Experience Points
6	+3	+1	14	+4	22	3
Attributes: Allergy to Cold Iron and Enchanted, Eyeless, Large, Lunge, Gatecrasher, Rock Hurler, Very Strong						
Equipment: Endless snapping mouths (Hand Weapon)						

GRIZZLY BEAR

These large and aggressive bears are especially territorial when either with their young or when attempting to put on fat before hibernating through the long, cold winters. Best left alone, they are sometimes hunted for food and their immensely warm pelts, and are often sent as emissaries or guards by the spirits that the colonists have disturbed in their often-clumsy expansion.

GRIZZLY BEAR						
Speed	Melee	Accuracy	Defence	Courage	Health	Experience Points
6	+2	+0	13	+2	16	2
Attributes: Large, Lunge, Strong						
Equipment: Fangs and Claws (Hand Weapon)						

HARVESTMAN AGENT

The lure of supernatural power and the ambitions of what riches the New World holds tempts many to follow the instructions of the dark powers rising in the Old World. Outfitted with objects and rituals to fulfil their goals, these Agents sow chaos and discord wherever they go.

HARVESTMAN AGENT						
Speed	Melee	Accuracy	Defence	Courage	Health	Experience Points
6	+0	+2	13	+2	12	2
Attributes: Curse Thrower (Wasting, Burning, Slowing)						
Equipment: Knife						

HARVESTMAN ASSASSIN

The forces of the Harvestmen have learned the hard way how much damage specialist units can inflict on their machinations. In an effort to limit such damage, they have recruited mortal agents and trained them to infiltrate and eliminate specialist officers while pitting the forces of different nations against each other. These Assassins are existential threats to the special units themselves.

HARVESTMAN ASSASSIN						
Speed	Melee	Accuracy	Defence	Courage	Health	Experience Points
6	+2	+2	14	+3	14	3
Attributes: Curse Thrower (Burning, Slowing)						
Equipment: Hand Weapon						

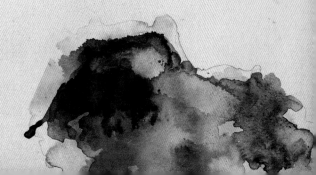

MOOSE

Though non-aggressive most of the year, the massive, gangly, and incredibly powerful moose was both a food source and occasional hazard to exploration in Canada. During a rut, males could easily trample and kill with their massive horns and immense weight, and the sheer size of these enormous cervines was shocking to European settlers.

MOOSE						
Speed	Melee	Accuracy	Defence	Courage	Health	Experience Points
7	+2	+0	13	+1	20	2
Attributes: Large, Strong, Non-Aggressive, Trample						
Equipment: Massive Horns and Hooves (Hand Weapon)						

POLAR BEAR

The great white bears of the Arctic are the largest land-based predators in North America. Often hunted for their meat by members of the Discovery Service, these same men could often run afoul of these apex predators as they clumsily made their way through the inhospitable Arctic.

POLAR BEAR						
Speed	Melee	Accuracy	Defence	Courage	Health	Experience Points
7	+3	+0	14	+2	18	3
Attributes: Large, Lunge, Strong, Trample						
Equipment: Fangs and Claws (Hand Weapon)						

TSEMAUS

The tsemaus is a spirit of the water that causes snags and disruption to those natural paths through the wilderness and becomes agitated and angry when feeling harassed by the passage of conflict. It can vary enormously in appearance, camouflaging itself from above as a cluster of debris, such as a log-jam or beaver-house, only to erupt as the yawning mouth of a bear, killer whale, or enormous frog from below. It can take the form of an amalgam of these things and can be terrifying to behold.

TSEMAUS						
Speed	Melee	Accuracy	Defence	Courage	Health	Experience Points
5	+3	+0	13	+3	20	3
Attributes: Allergy to Fire, Aquatic, Damage Reduction (2), Large, Strong, Master of Cover, Lunge, Swimmer						
Equipment: Gaping Jaws and Crushing Fns (Hand Weapon)						

WENDIGO

The Wendigo is a malevolent spirit said to inhabit those to have engaged in cannibalism or other such despicable acts. The afflicted experience a ravenous and insatiable hunger that can never actually be sated, as they grow more gaunt and emaciated no matter what and how much they eat. They instead grow proportionally to the victims they consume and can become towering monstrosities of sinew and talons that will commit ever escalating atrocities until they are destroyed in an attempt to sate their endless obsession with feeding.

WENDIGO						
Speed	Melee	Accuracy	Defence	Courage	Health	Experience Points
7	+3	+0	14	+4	16	3
Attributes: Allergy to Fire & Blessed, Damage Reduction (4), Large, Strong, Master of Cover, Lunge						
Equipment: Rending Talons (Hand Weapon)						

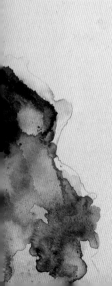

CHAPTER SIX

NEW ATTRIBUTES

AQUATIC

This figure naturally inhabits water and will not leave a water terrain feature but will still take the quickest route possible through one to reach their target point.

> Designer's Note: The Lunge ability may be used for an Aquatic creature to attack another figure not in water terrain.

CURSETHROWER

This figure throws cursed objects, which count as a Shooting Attack with a range of 10". It can run out of ammunition and will need to be reloaded as normal (the figure searches for more ingredients to be thrown, rather than having to actually 'reload' an object). The nature of the curse will dictate the effects if it should hit:

- Wasting: It causes no initial Damage, but that figure will take 1 point of Damage each time they activate from now on as the curse draws out their life. If the cursing figure is not slain, then the curse causes the figure to automatically have to make an injury roll at the conclusion of the scenario.
- Burning: Power Die +1 Damage – Roll D10 for each other figure within 3", on a 7+ they take D5 Damage.
- Slowing: It causes no damage. The figure hit halves all movement until they can pass a TN 11 Courage Test at the start of a following activation.

Each time a figure throws a curse, randomise which effect they have chosen (if they have access to all of them, for instance, roll a D3).

EYELESS

This figure relies on other senses to hunt its prey and does not require line of sight to the closest figure to target it.

FIRESTARTER(O)

This figure may replace either a Move or Shoot action to swap one item of Specialist Equipment it is carrying with Oil and Torches. After the game, they return to their normal equipment.

GATECRASHER

This figure completely ignores movement penalties for low walls, obstacles, and gates, instead simply crashing through them. Mark an area equal to the base size of this figure once it passes through an obstacle or remove the obstacle from the table if it is narrower than the figure's base as it is crushed to insignificance. This area may be passed through freely from now on, incurring no movement penalties.

LUNGE(O)

This figure may spend an action to fight a round of melee against a target within 1" instead of needing to be in contact. The combat is resolved as normal. If this model has the Large attribute as well, it may do so within 2" of its target instead. This may be measured vertically as well as horizontally from the tallest reasonable point of the model.

NON-AGGRESSIVE

This figure will only become aggressive if it feels threatened. When it appears on a table edge it will move in a straight line towards the opposite edge, leaving once it can move off. If a firearm is fired within 12" of it, or it begins an activation with a soldier within 6" of it, it will immediately become aggressive and target that model until either one is destroyed. It will then continue to follow the wandering monster rules as normal after that. If left alone, it will simply leave the battlefield.

SWIMMER(O)

This figure does not count any water terrain feature as difficult ground and, when in water, may choose to count as being in cover. If it ever uses a water terrain feature as cover during the course of a game however, it may no longer use any ranged weapons for the duration of the encounter as they become fouled with water.

TRAMPLE

If this figure strikes a model in melee that is of a smaller size (i.e. a Large model striking a model without Large), it will knock it down in addition to doing Damage. A knocked-down figure must forfeit its move action to stand up during its following activation and, if defending from a melee attack while knocked-down, will suffer -2 Defence.

CREDITS

I would like to thank all of my indigenous and First Nations hosts for their hospitality and friendship. Thank you as well to my friends and family for their support and to my Editor Phil for his endless patience.

AUTHOR

Ash Barker discovered miniatures in 1988 in the back of the classic *Fighting Fantasy* adventure books. These tiny, perfect worlds and their heroic inhabitants would capture his imagination for the next 30 years. Since 2001 he has worked in the wargames industry. In June 2015 he founded Guerrilla Miniature Games, a YouTube channel that specialises in bringing a spotlight to all miniature games, great and small.

ILLUSTRATOR

Brainbug Design is a 2D conceptual art, illustration, and visual development studio embedded within the entertainment industries. Based in Nottingham, UK, Brainbug was founded in 2018 by industry veterans with over 30 years' combined experience and one singular goal: to burrow deep into intellectual properties to provide the best possible external symbiosis with the host-client! Deeply passionate about world-building and storytelling through the medium of design, Brainbug has collaborated on everything from film and television to giant AAA titles and compact independent video games.

THE SILVER BAYONET

OFFICIAL MINIATURES AVAILABLE FROM

Nick Eyre's
NORTH STAR
Military Figures

WWW.NORTHSTARFIGURES.COM